Summer holidays
- D.C.

For Roslyn
- B.O'D.

For Gran
- B.L.

First published in Ireland by Discovery Publications, Brookfield Business Centre,
333 Crumlin Road, Belfast BT14 7EA
Telephone: 028 9049 2410
Email address: declan.carville@ntlworld.com

A CIP catalogue record of this book is available from the British Library.

Printed in Belgium by Proost NV. Turnhout.

ISBN 0-9538222-3-0

1 2 3 4 5 6 7 8 9 10

THE Fairy Glen

Declan Carville

illustrated by Belinda Larmour

book design by Bernard O'Donnell

Let me tell you about a special place.
The Fairy Glen, in the Kingdom of Mourne.

You will find a little cottage
near to where the river flows,
Take a skip over the bridge
and follow the path where it goes.

They come out when it is dark
and there is no one around,
Five, maybe six
they hardly make a sound.

No bigger than a hand
and every colour you could wish,
Look! Over there, beside the evergreen bush!

Kathleen is small and must be careful how she goes,

Not like her friend Deirdre who dashes on tiptoes.

The boys are full of mischief
though Tom keeps a watchful eye,

Little Mary is the youngest

and not quite ready yet to fly.

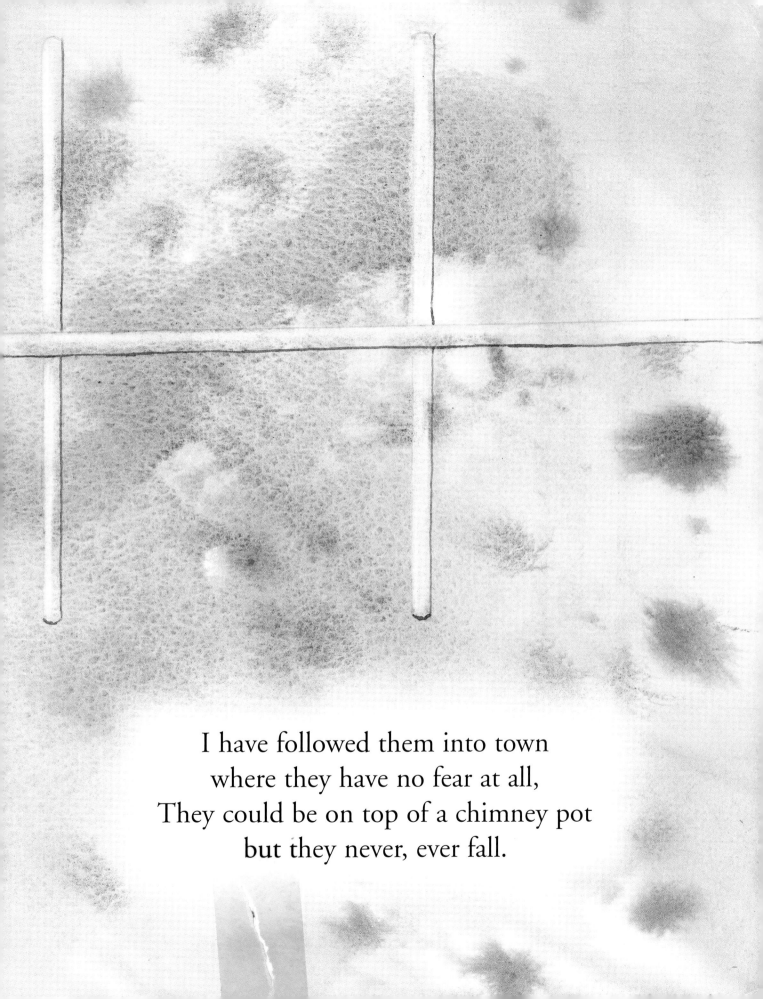

I have followed them into town
where they have no fear at all,
They could be on top of a chimney pot
but they never, ever fall.

Sometimes they are quite happy
to hum their merry little tune,
Join hands and dance in circles
under the light of the moon.

Until they fall in a heap
with their legs kicking in the air,
I wonder what would happen
if they could see me stare!

They love to explore when there is no one around,

And gaze into windows at the things to be found.

Maybe a trip to the forest
to visit a few friends,
Until the first break of light
when their adventure must end.

Time to go back as the darkness slowly dies...

I tell you I have seen it all with my very own eyes.

Fairy Glen

The Fairy Glen is to be found in Rostrevor, County Down, Ireland
at the foot of the Mourne Mountains.